LEGO Disney **PRINCESS**

The FRIENDSHIP Bridge

Written by
Laura Buller

Illustrated by the
Ameet Studio Artists

Copyright © 2018 Disney Enterprises, Inc. All rights reserved. Published by Disney Press, an imprint of Disney Book Group. No part of this book may be reproduced or transmitted in any form or by any means, electronic or mechanical, including photocopying, recording, or by any information storage and retrieval system, without written permission from the publisher. For information address Disney Press, 1200 Grand Central Avenue, Glendale, California 91201.
First Paperback Edition, October 2018
1 3 5 7 9 10 8 6 4 2
ISBN 978-1-368-02305-4
FAC-029261-18257
Library of Congress Control Number: 2018936733
Printed in the United States of America
For more Disney Press fun, visit www.disneybooks.com

SUSTAINABLE
FORESTRY
INITIATIVE
Certified Sourcing
www.sfiprogram.org
SFI-01415

There is a girl who loves to build with her LEGO bricks.

She built all the princess castles. Then she put them together. She made a big new castle. It is magical.

The girl loves the Disney Princesses, too. She put them in the castle. Now she makes up stories about them.

This is one of her stories. . . .

Splish-splash. Raindrops fall on the roof of the magical castle. It has been raining all day.

Will it ever stop raining? thinks Rapunzel. *I know the rain is good for the orchard and the flowers. But we want to go outside! I can't stay in this tower forever.*

There is so much rain. The little stream between the castle and the flower gardens is a big stream now!

Belle rushes in the front door.
She has been walking the
puppy.

"My dress is all soggy again!"
she says. "Ariel, I know you
love the water, but I don't like
getting so wet."

The puppy shakes its body, and water flies everywhere. Ariel gives the puppy a hug. "Oh! Now don't make it rain inside, too!" she says.

"I know. Let's ask the dragon to help!" says Ariel. "She's up on the roof. Maybe she can blow away the rain clouds."

The dragon huffs and puffs, but the rain keeps falling. Down, down, down it pours. The little stream looks more like a big river!

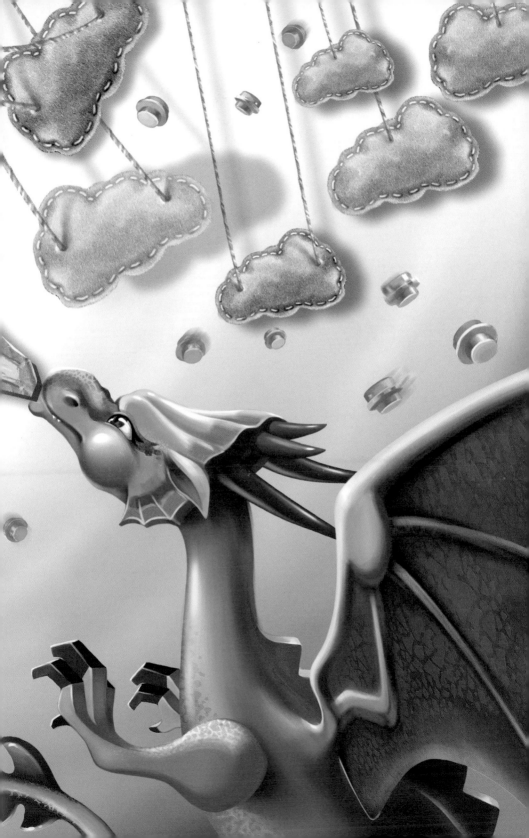

Cinderella says, "We need a different plan. Let's put our heads together. Rain, rain, go away. The princesses want to play!"

Finally, the rain stops! But the stream is a river now. How will the princesses get across it to smell the flowers and see the butterflies?

Rapunzel has an idea. "I know!
When you have a problem you
have to get over, then you need
a bridge!" she says. "We can
use my hair."

Belle giggles. "That's so funny. But why don't we build a real bridge?"

The princesses make a plan. They will build a bridge from each side that meets in the middle.

First some of the princesses
need to get across the river.
The water is so high it bubbles
up the banks. "Ariel, I think you
should go first," says Mulan.
"Make a splash!"

Ariel jumps in. She uses her mermaid skills. *Splash!* She swims to the other bank in a flash.

"Why did Ariel cross the river?" she jokes with her friends. "To get to the other side! Come on over, Mulan!"

Mulan spots some stepping-stones in the water. She leaps from one flat rock to the next to meet Ariel. It's tricky, but she doesn't slip!

"Look! I'm a *rock* star!" she exclaims.

Aurora is next. *Hmmm* . . . she thinks. *I can't fly like a bird, but I can climb very high.* She scrambles up a tree. She is such a good climber! Aurora swings through the branches and lands next to her friends.

Belle and Rapunzel think about
what the bridge will look like.
"I read about a beautiful bridge
in a fairy tale once," Belle
says. "Let's make our bridge
magical!"

The princesses build the bridge one brick at a time. The puppy leaps around their feet, barking happily. He can't wait to be the first to dash across.

The puppy rushes right up to
the gap between the two halves
of the bridge. "Careful, Puppy!
Better pause your paws!" says
Aurora.

Ta-da! The last brick is in place. The bridge is complete! And the sun comes out. A beautiful rainbow appears in the sky.

"We don't need this bridge after all," Belle jokes with her friends. "We can climb right over that rainbow and slide down!"

"I'll ride across on that fluffy cloud," adds Rapunzel.

There's just one more thing to do! The princesses want the bridge to be as beautiful as the rest of the castle. They decorate it with colored jewels and bright flowers.

"Let's call this Friendship Bridge!" says Rapunzel. "Now we can visit the gardens whatever the weather. Friends can do anything when we work together!"

"So let's find the end of the rainbow," says Cinderella.